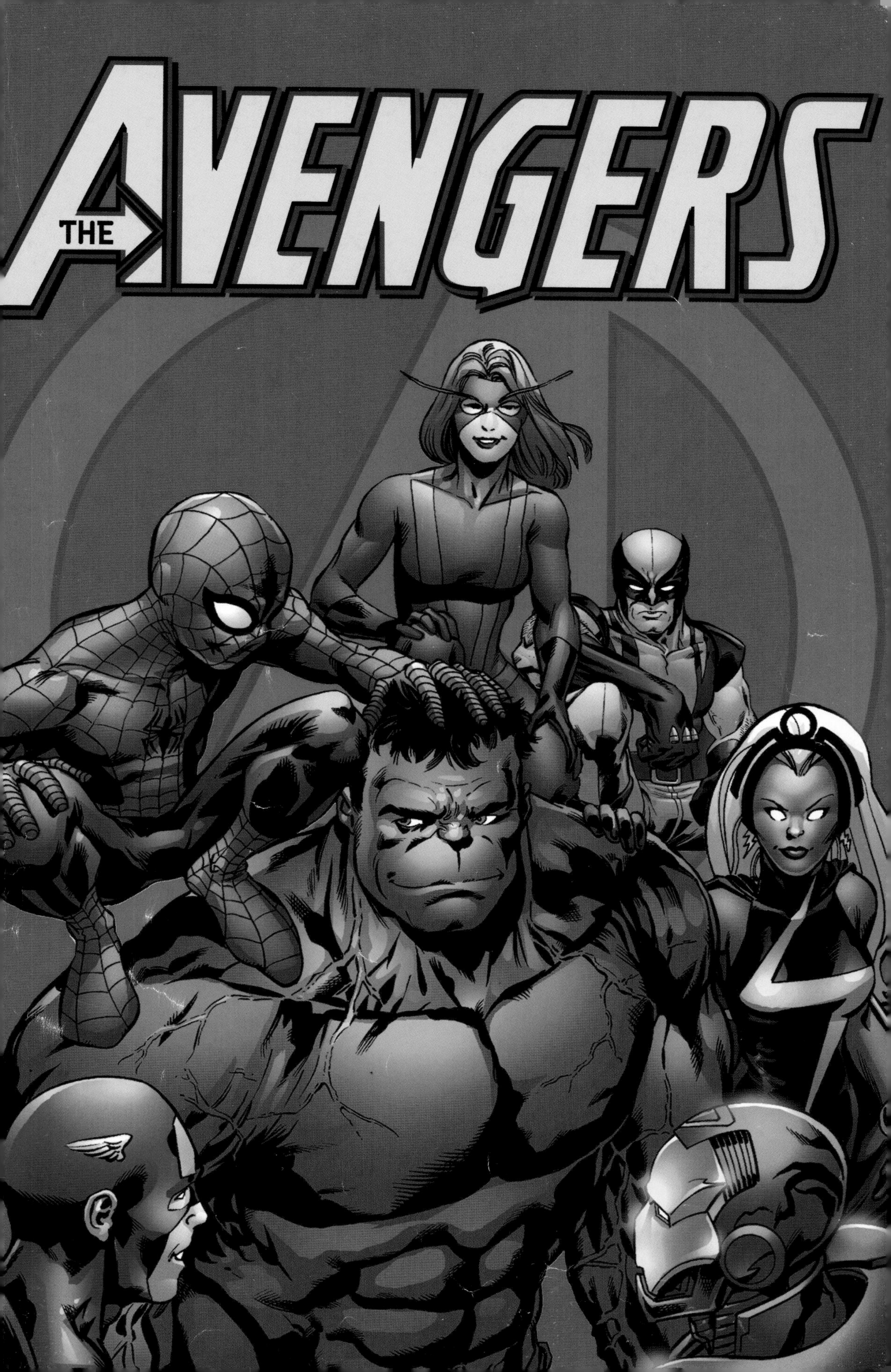
THE AVENGERS

VISIT US AT
www.abdopublishing.com

Reinforced library bound edition published in 2011 by Spotlight, a division of the ABDO Group, 8000 West 78th Street, Edina, Minnesota 55439. Spotlight produces high-quality reinforced library bound editions for schools and libraries. Published by agreement with Marvel Characters, Inc.

Printed in the United States of America, Melrose Park, Illinois.
042010
092010
 This book contains at least 10% recycled material.

Library of Congress Cataloging-in-Publication Data

Tobin, Paul.
  Ms. Isaacson's third grade field trip / story, Paul Tobin ; art, Jacopo Camagni.
    p. cm. -- (The Avengers)
"Marvel."
  ISBN 978-1-59961-768-8
  1. Graphic novels. I. Camagni, Jacopo, ill. II. Avengers (Comic strip) III. Title.
  PZ7.7.T62Ms 2010
  741.5'973--dc22
                        2009052834

All Spotlight books have reinforced library bindings and are manufactured in the United States of America.

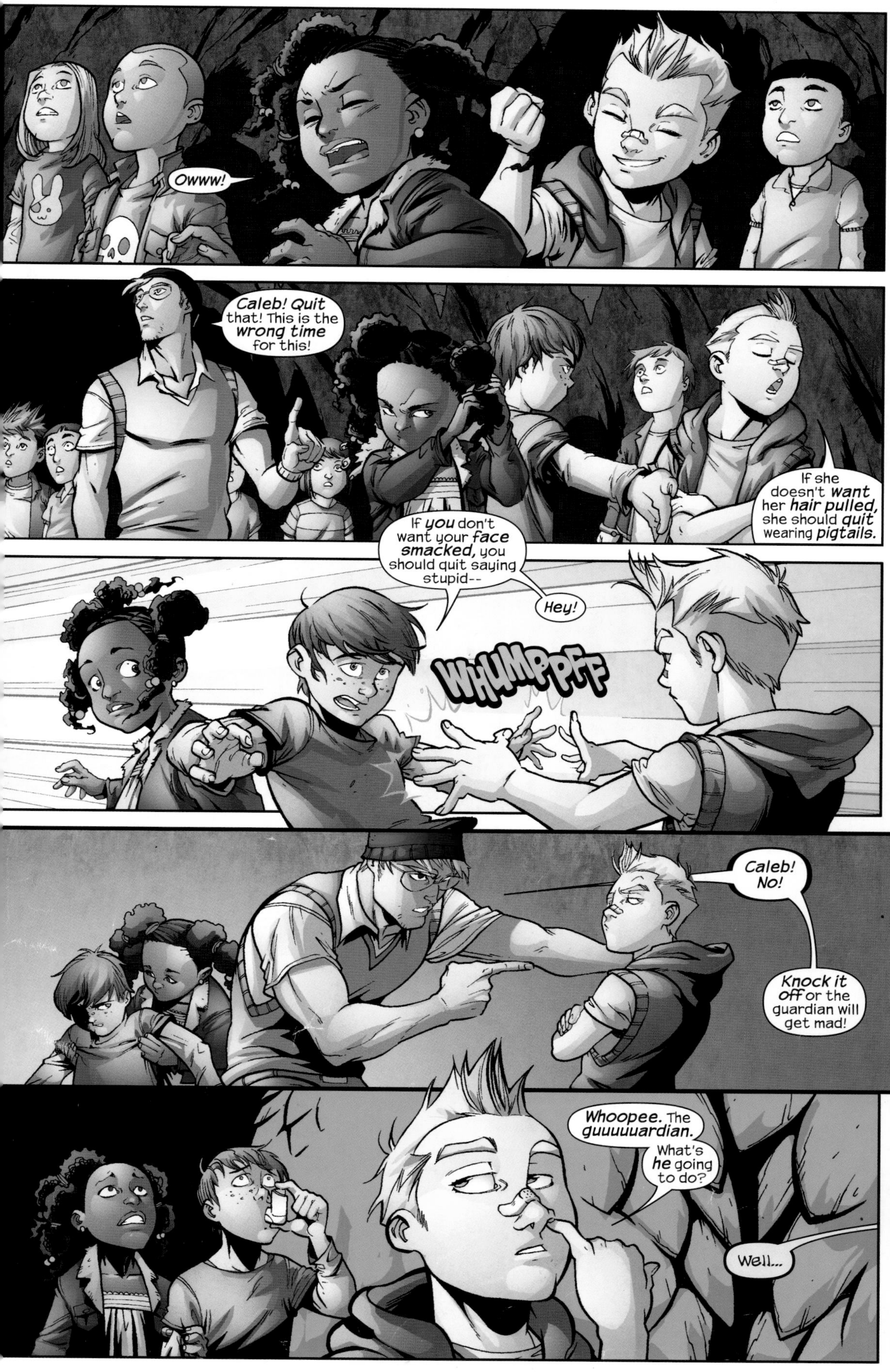
Owww!
Caleb! Quit that! This is the wrong time for this!
If she doesn't want her hair pulled, she should quit wearing pigtails.
If you don't want your face smacked, you should quit saying stupid--
Hey!
WHUMPPFF
Caleb! No!
Knock it off or the guardian will get mad!
Whoopee. The guuuuuardian.
What's he going to do?
Well...

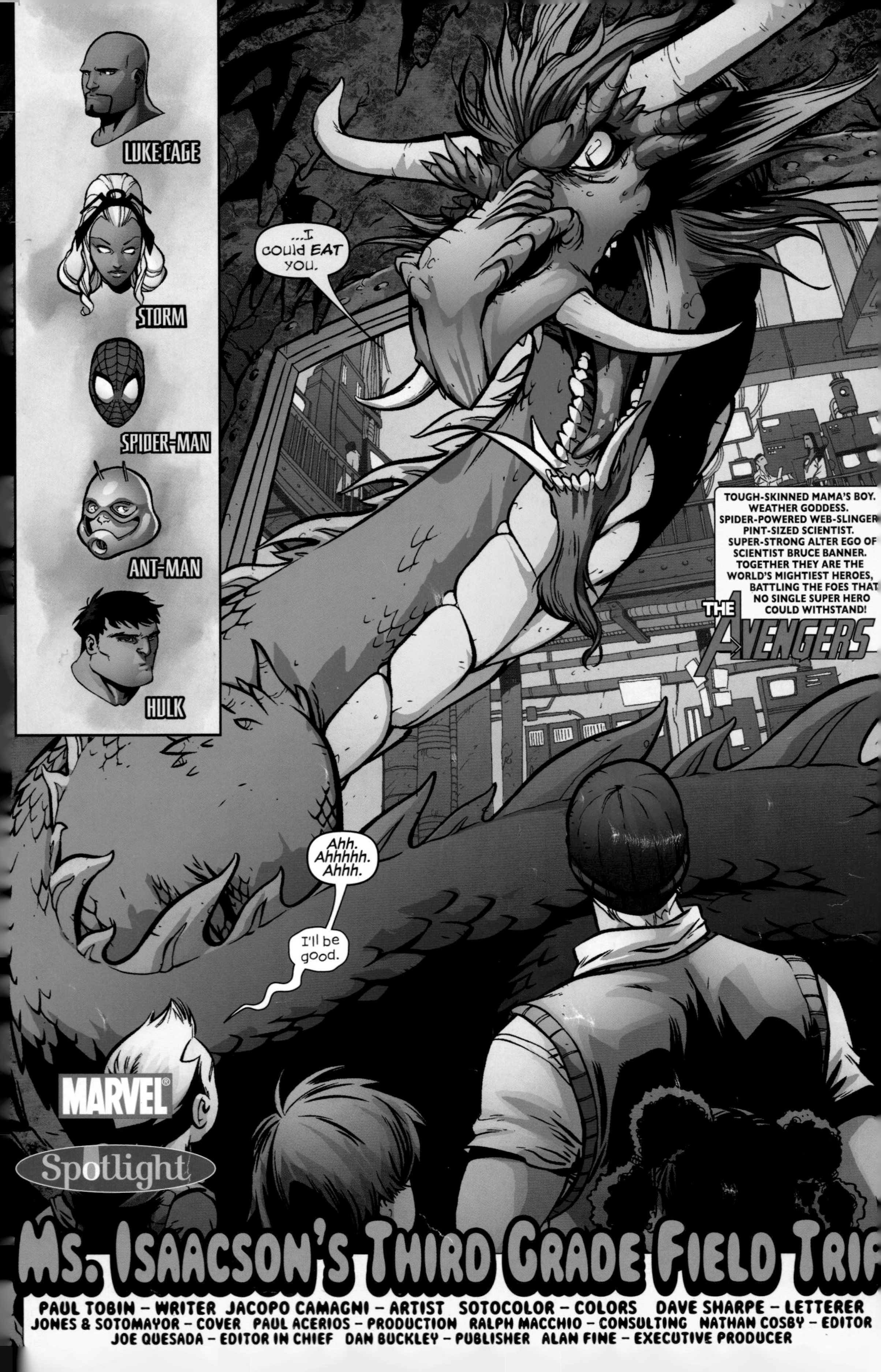

LUKE CAGE
STORM
SPIDER-MAN
ANT-MAN
HULK
...I could EAT you.
TOUGH-SKINNED MAMA'S BOY. WEATHER GODDESS. SPIDER-POWERED WEB-SLINGER. PINT-SIZED SCIENTIST. SUPER-STRONG ALTER EGO OF SCIENTIST BRUCE BANNER. TOGETHER THEY ARE THE WORLD'S MIGHTIEST HEROES, BATTLING THE FOES THAT NO SINGLE SUPER HERO COULD WITHSTAND!
THE AVENGERS
Ahh. Ahhhhh. Ahhh.
I'll be good.
MARVEL
Spotlight
MS. ISAACSON'S THIRD GRADE FIELD TRIP
PAUL TOBIN – WRITER JACOPO CAMAGNI – ARTIST SOTOCOLOR – COLORS DAVE SHARPE – LETTERER
JONES & SOTOMAYOR – COVER PAUL ACERIOS – PRODUCTION RALPH MACCHIO – CONSULTING NATHAN COSBY – EDITOR
JOE QUESADA – EDITOR IN CHIEF DAN BUCKLEY – PUBLISHER ALAN FINE – EXECUTIVE PRODUCER

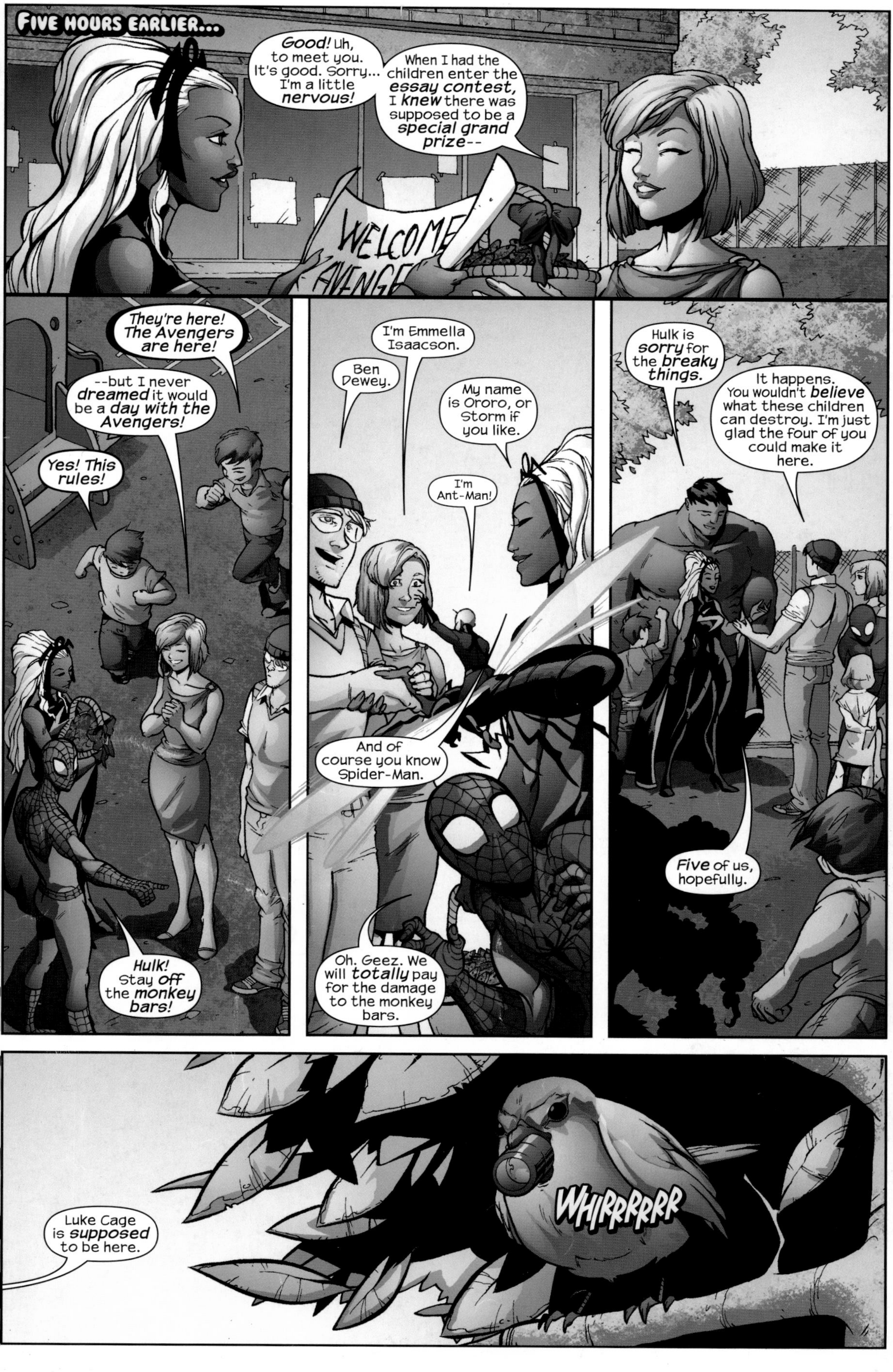
FIVE HOURS EARLIER...
Good! Uh, to meet you. It's good. Sorry... I'm a little nervous!
When I had the children enter the essay contest, I knew there was supposed to be a special grand prize--
WELCOME AVENGE
They're here! The Avengers are here!
--but I never dreamed it would be a day with the Avengers!
Yes! This rules!
Hulk! Stay off the monkey bars!
I'm Emmella Isaacson.
Ben Dewey.
My name is Ororo, or Storm if you like.
I'm Ant-Man!
And of course you know Spider-Man.
Oh. Geez. We will totally pay for the damage to the monkey bars.
Hulk is sorry for the breaky things.
It happens. You wouldn't believe what these children can destroy. I'm just glad the four of you could make it here.
Five of us, hopefully.
Luke Cage is supposed to be here.
WHIRRRRRR

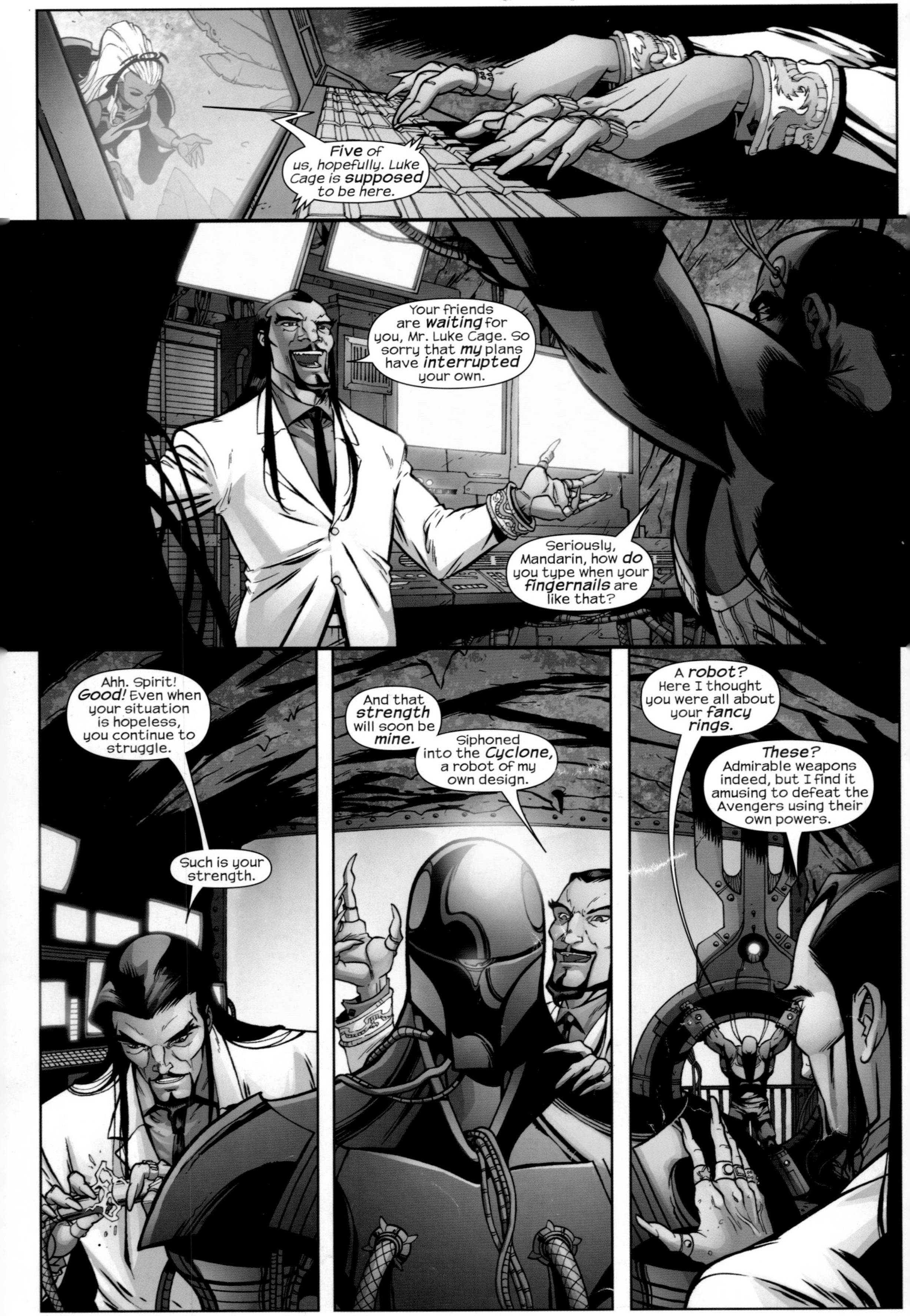
Five of us, hopefully. Luke Cage is supposed to be here.
Your friends are waiting for you, Mr. Luke Cage. So sorry that my plans have interrupted your own.
Seriously, Mandarin, how do you type when your fingernails are like that?
Ahh. Spirit! Good! Even when your situation is hopeless, you continue to struggle.
Such is your strength.
And that strength will soon be mine.
Siphoned into the Cyclone, a robot of my own design.
A robot? Here I thought you were all about your fancy rings.
These? Admirable weapons indeed, but I find it amusing to defeat the Avengers using their own powers.

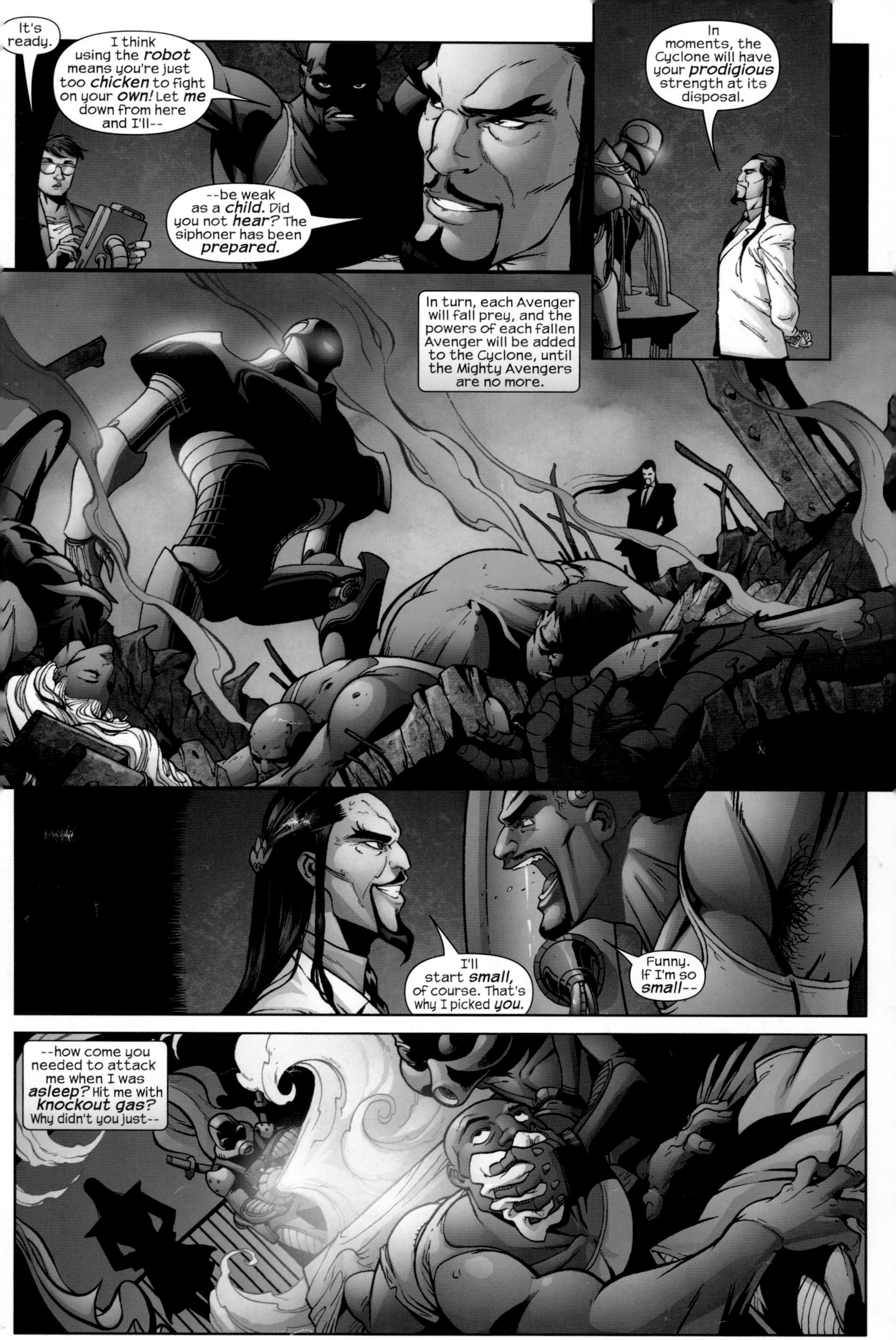
It's ready.
I think using the robot means you're just too chicken to fight on your own! Let me down from here and I'll--
--be weak as a child. Did you not hear? The siphoner has been prepared.
In moments, the Cyclone will have your prodigious strength at its disposal.
In turn, each Avenger will fall prey, and the powers of each fallen Avenger will be added to the Cyclone, until the Mighty Avengers are no more.
I'll start small, of course. That's why I picked you.
Funny. If I'm so small--
--how come you needed to attack me when I was asleep? Hit me with knockout gas? Why didn't you just--

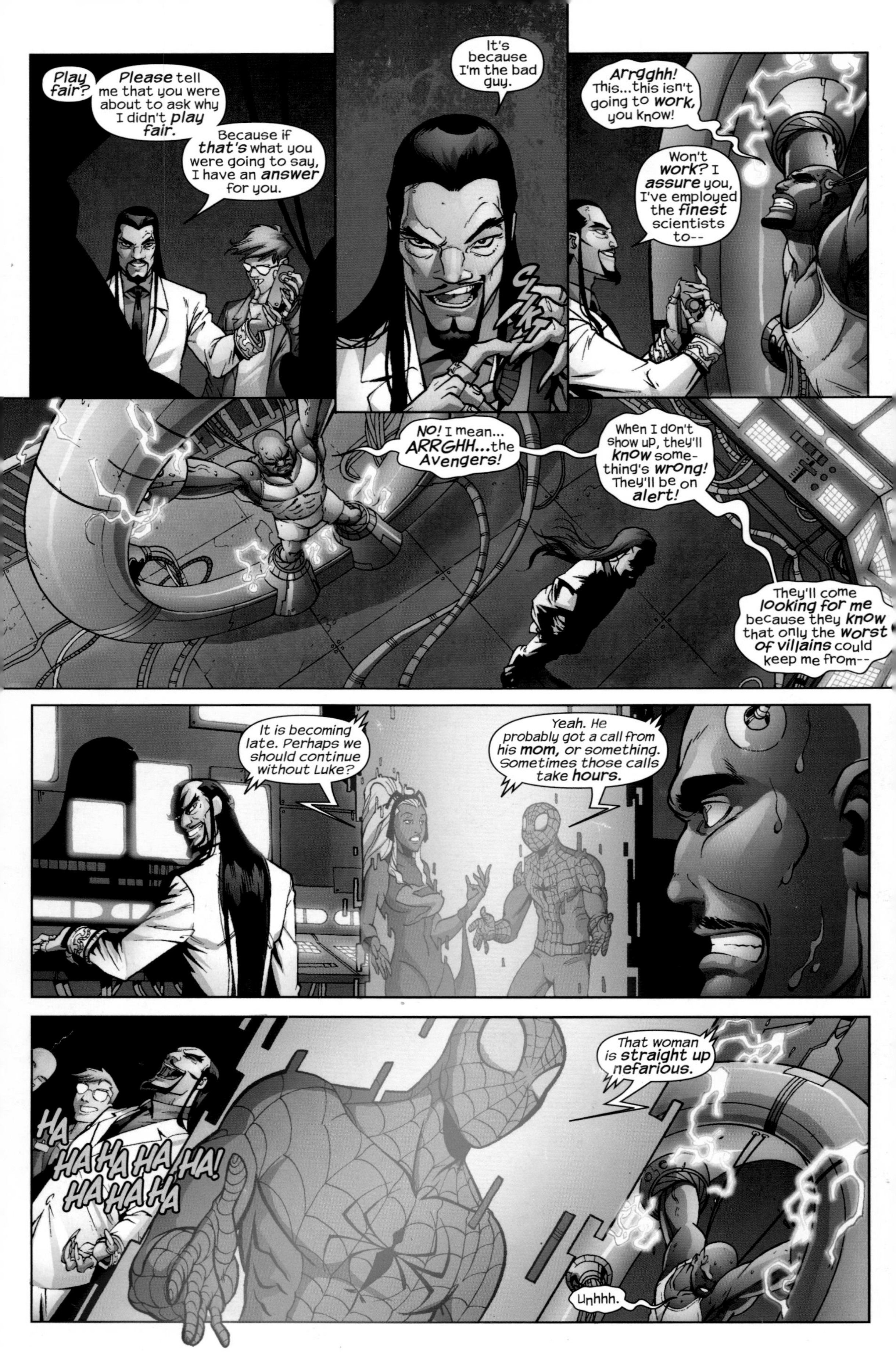
Play fair?
Please tell me that you were about to ask why I didn't play fair.
Because if that's what you were going to say, I have an answer for you.
It's because I'm the bad guy.
CLIK
Arrgghh! This...this isn't going to work, you know!
Won't work? I assure you, I've employed the finest scientists to--
NO! I mean... ARRGHH...the Avengers!
When I don't show up, they'll know something's wrong! They'll be on alert!
They'll come looking for me because they know that only the worst of villains could keep me from--
It is becoming late. Perhaps we should continue without Luke?
Yeah. He probably got a call from his mom, or something. Sometimes those calls take hours.
HA HA HA HA HA! HA HA HA
That woman is straight up nefarious.
Unhhh.

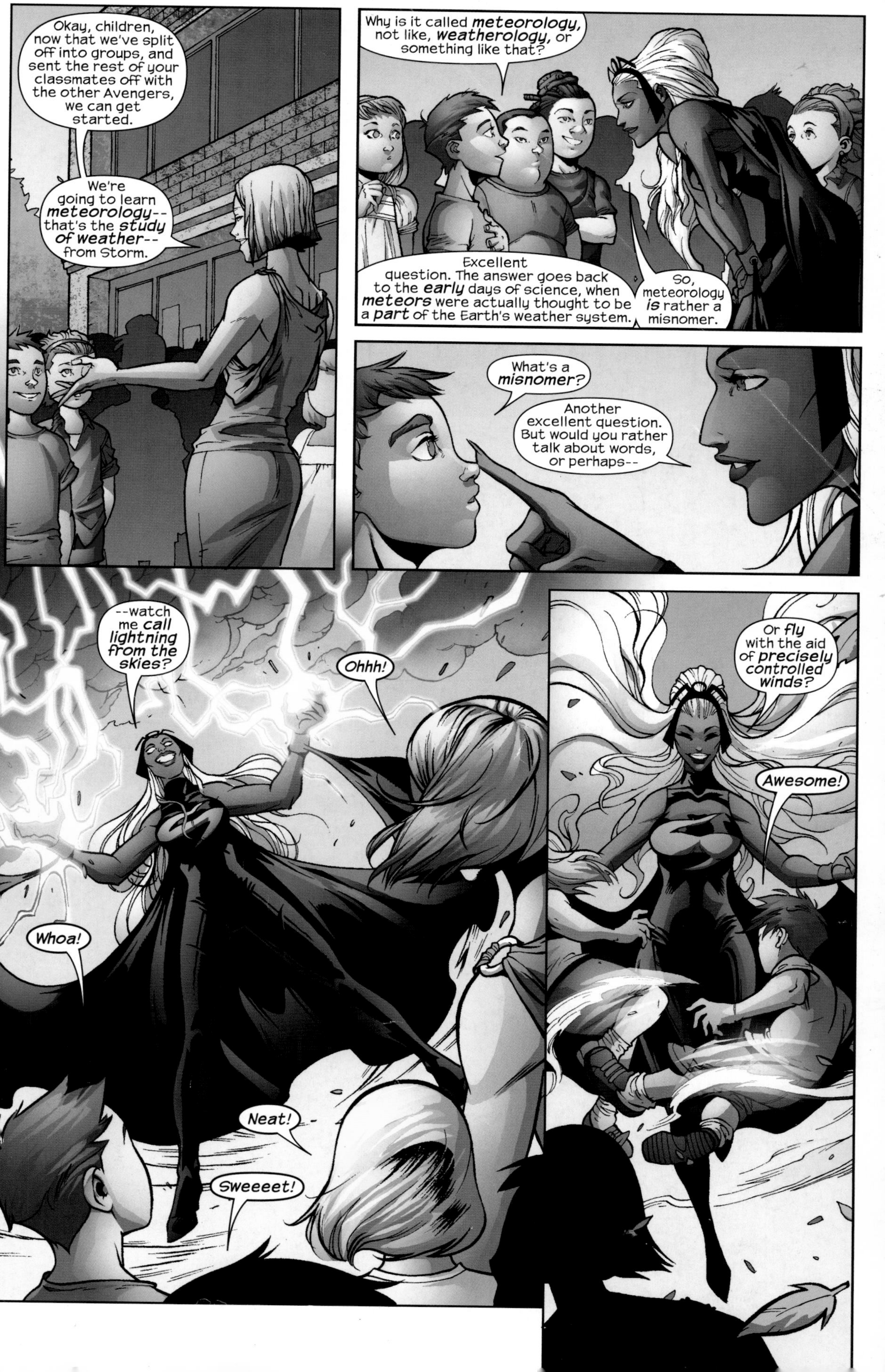
Okay, children, now that we've split off into groups, and sent the rest of your classmates off with the other Avengers, we can get started.
We're going to learn meteorology--that's the study of weather--from Storm.
Why is it called meteorology, not like, weatherology, or something like that?
Excellent question. The answer goes back to the early days of science, when meteors were actually thought to be a part of the Earth's weather system.
So, meteorology is rather a misnomer.
What's a misnomer?
Another excellent question. But would you rather talk about words, or perhaps--
--watch me call lightning from the skies?
Ohhh!
Whoa!
Neat!
Sweeeet!
Or fly with the aid of precisely controlled winds?
Awesome!

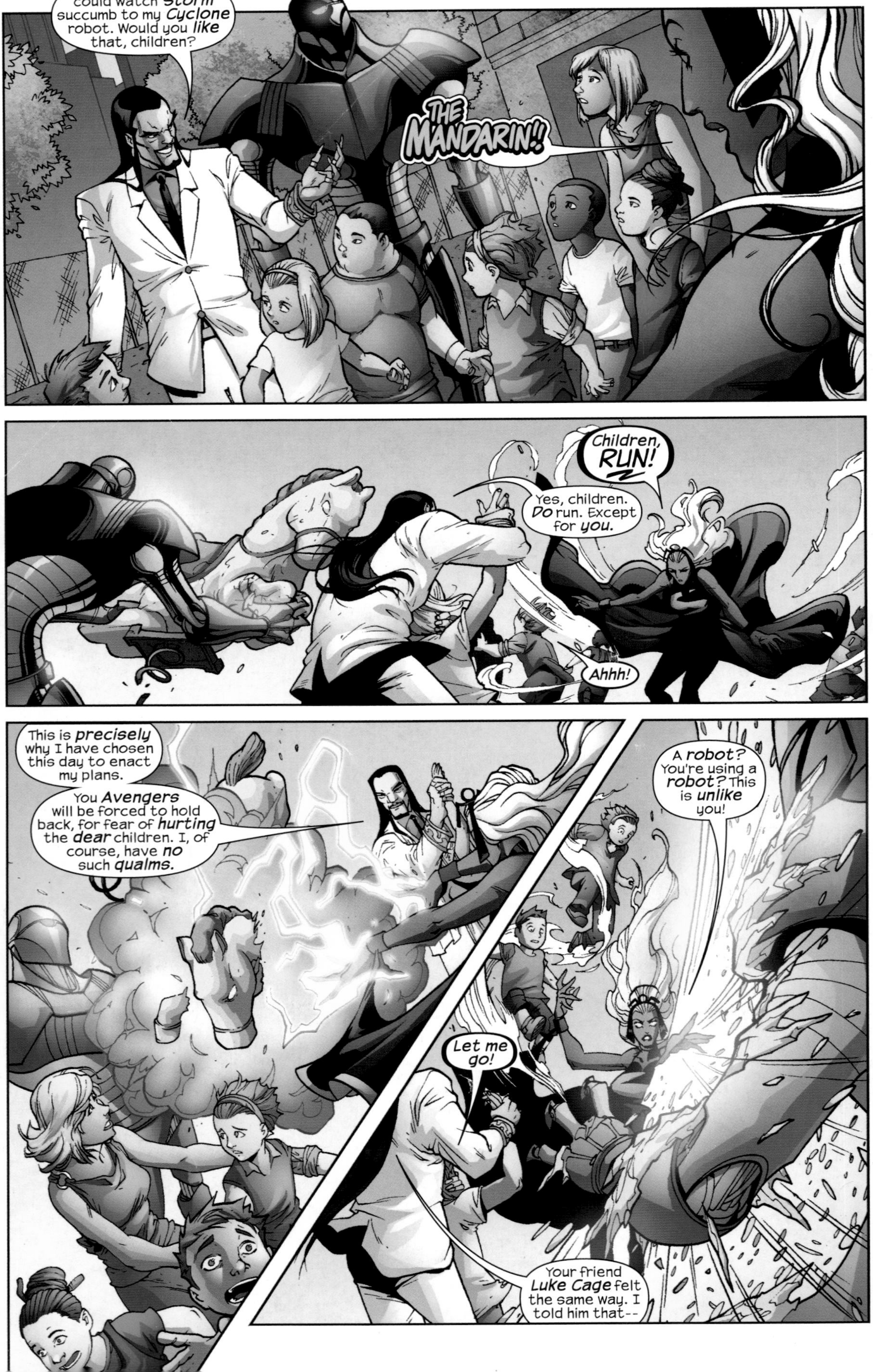

Or... you could watch Storm succumb to my Cyclone robot. Would you like that, children?
THE MANDARIN!!
Children, RUN!
Yes, children. Do run. Except for you.
Ahhh!
This is precisely why I have chosen this day to enact my plans.
You Avengers will be forced to hold back, for fear of hurting the dear children. I, of course, have no such qualms.
A robot? You're using a robot? This is unlike you!
Let me go!
Your friend Luke Cage felt the same way. I told him that--

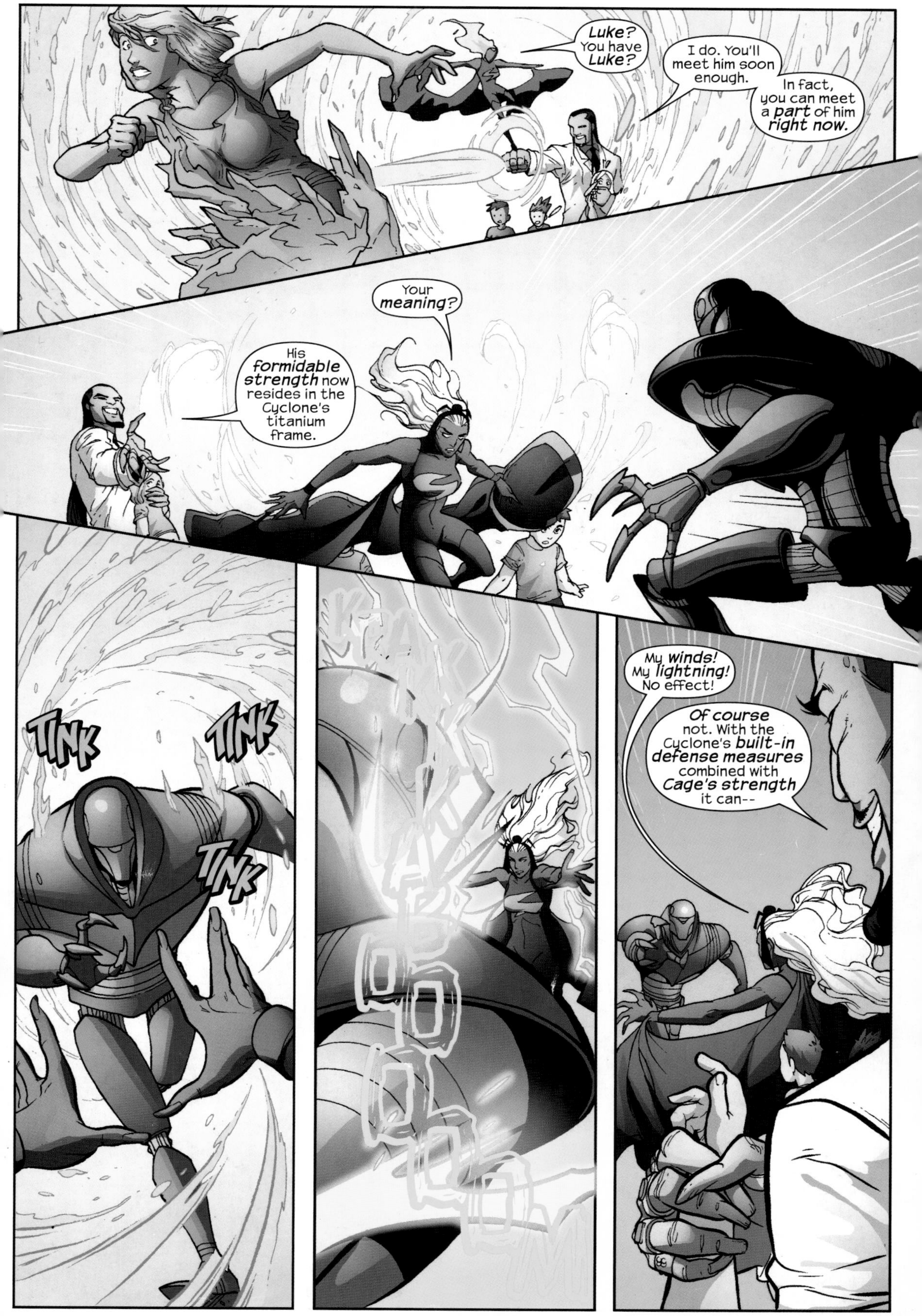

Luke? You have Luke?
I do. You'll meet him soon enough.
In fact, you can meet a part of him right now.
Your meaning?
His formidable strength now resides in the Cyclone's titanium frame.
TINK
TINK
TINK
My winds! My lightning! No effect!
Of course not. With the Cyclone's built-in defense measures combined with Cage's strength it can--

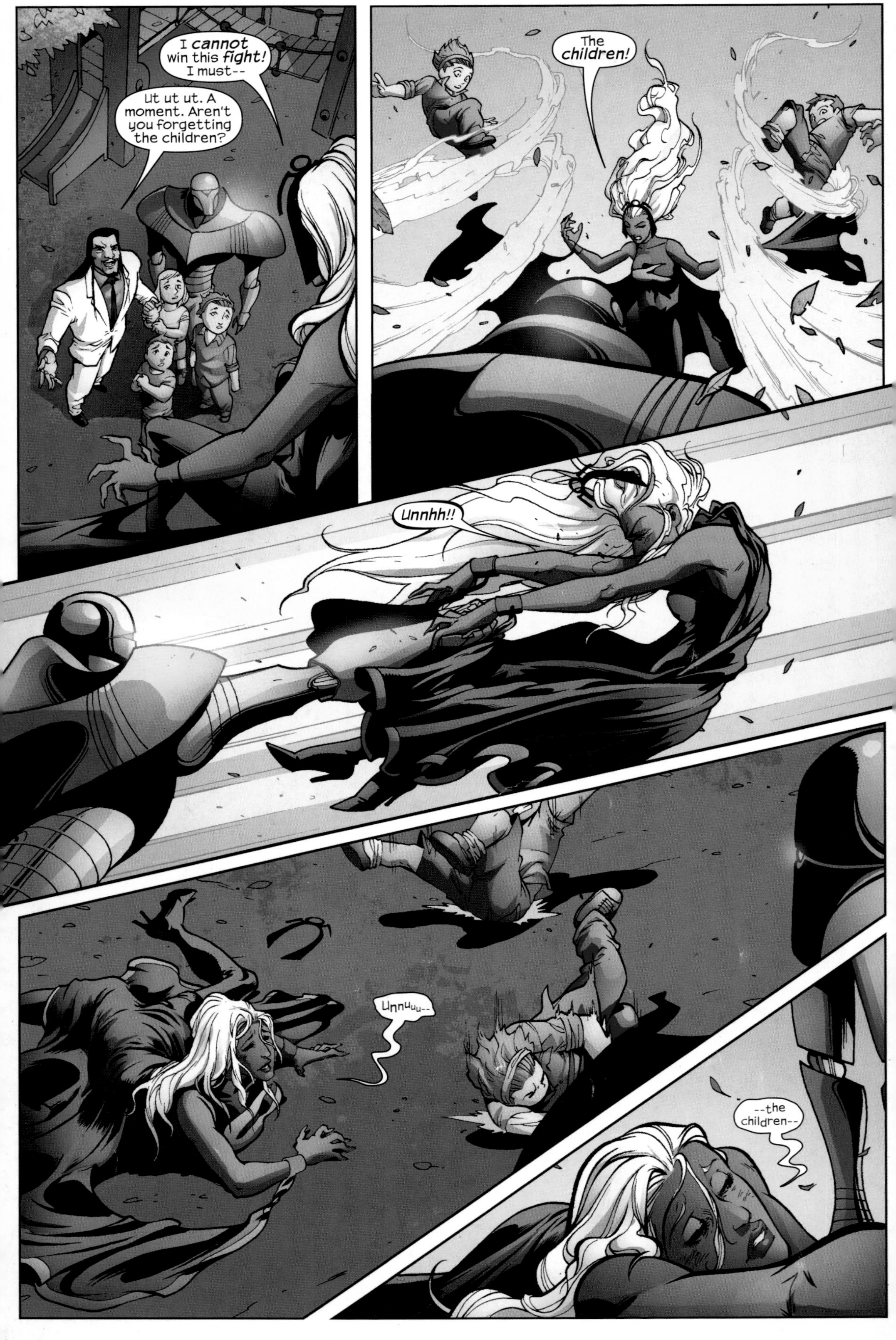
I cannot win this fight! I must--
Ut ut ut. A moment. Aren't you forgetting the children?
The children!
Unnhh!!
Unnuuu--
--the children--

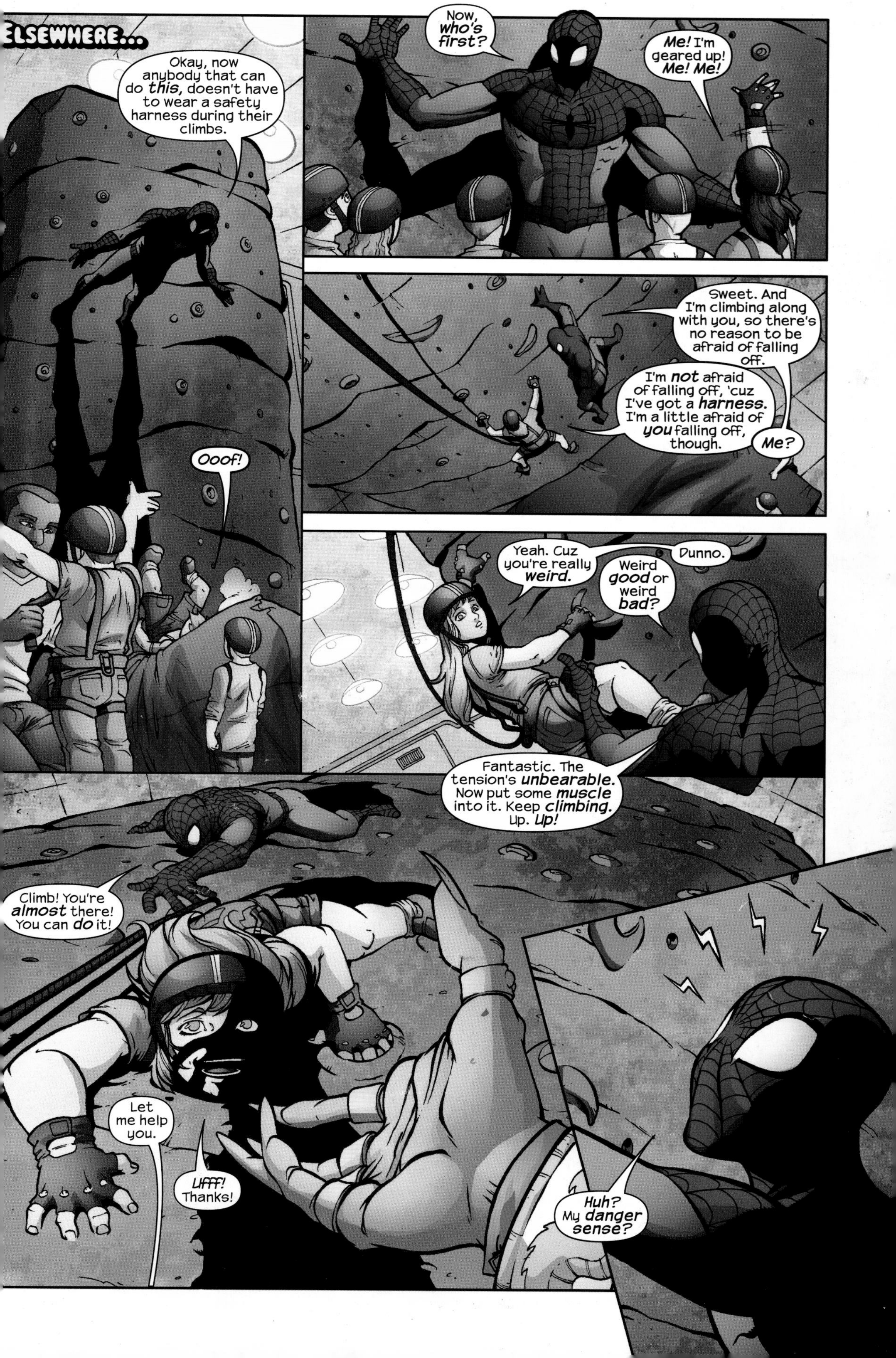
ELSEWHERE...
Okay, now anybody that can do this, doesn't have to wear a safety harness during their climbs.
Ooof!
Now, who's first?
Me! I'm geared up! Me! Me!
Sweet. And I'm climbing along with you, so there's no reason to be afraid of falling off.
I'm not afraid of falling off, 'cuz I've got a harness. I'm a little afraid of you falling off, though.
Me?
Yeah. Cuz you're really weird.
Weird good or weird bad?
Dunno.
Fantastic. The tension's unbearable. Now put some muscle into it. Keep climbing. Up. Up!
Climb! You're almost there! You can do it!
Let me help you.
Ufff! Thanks!
Huh? My danger sense?

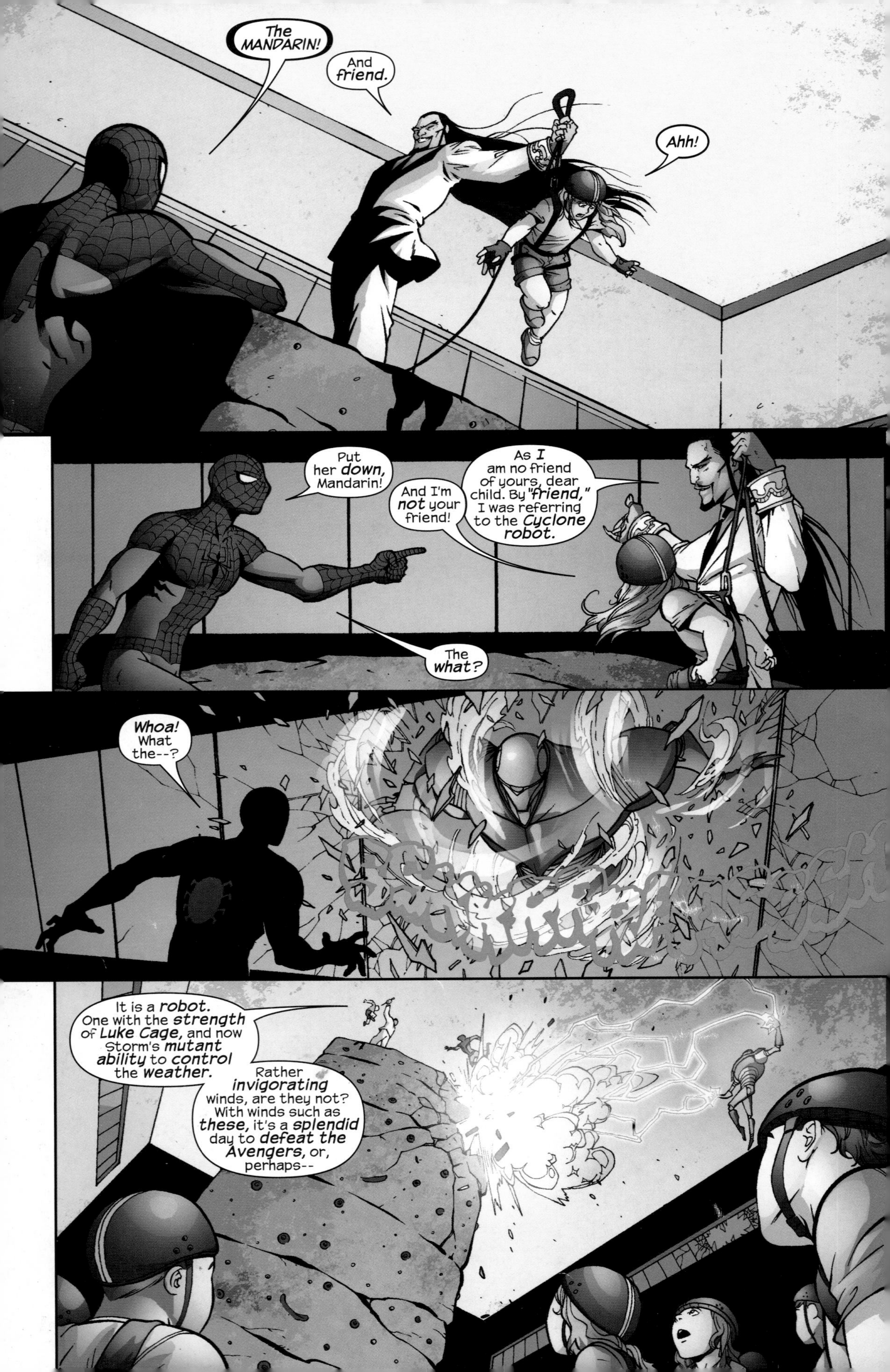

The MANDARIN!
And friend.
Ahh!
Put her down, Mandarin!
And I'm not your friend!
As I am no friend of yours, dear child. By "friend," I was referring to the Cyclone robot.
The what?
Whoa! What the--?
It is a robot. One with the strength of Luke Cage, and now Storm's mutant ability to control the weather.
Rather invigorating winds, are they not? With winds such as these, it's a splendid day to defeat the Avengers, or, perhaps--

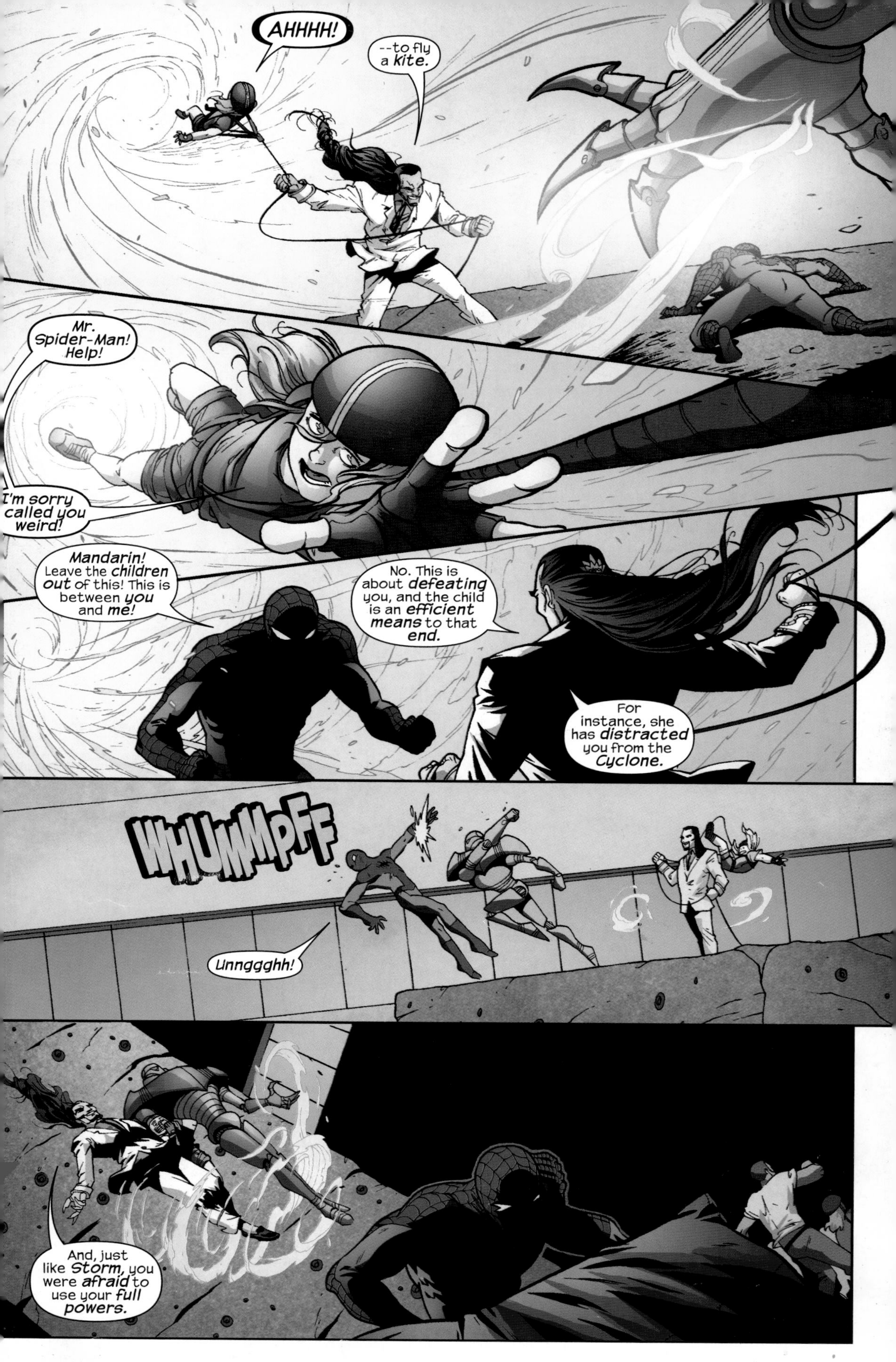
AHHHH!
--to fly a kite.
Mr. Spider-Man! Help!
I'm sorry called you weird!
Mandarin! Leave the children out of this! This is between you and me!
No. This is about defeating you, and the child is an efficient means to that end.
For instance, she has distracted you from the Cyclone.
WHUMMPFF
Unnggghh!
And, just like Storm, you were afraid to use your full powers.

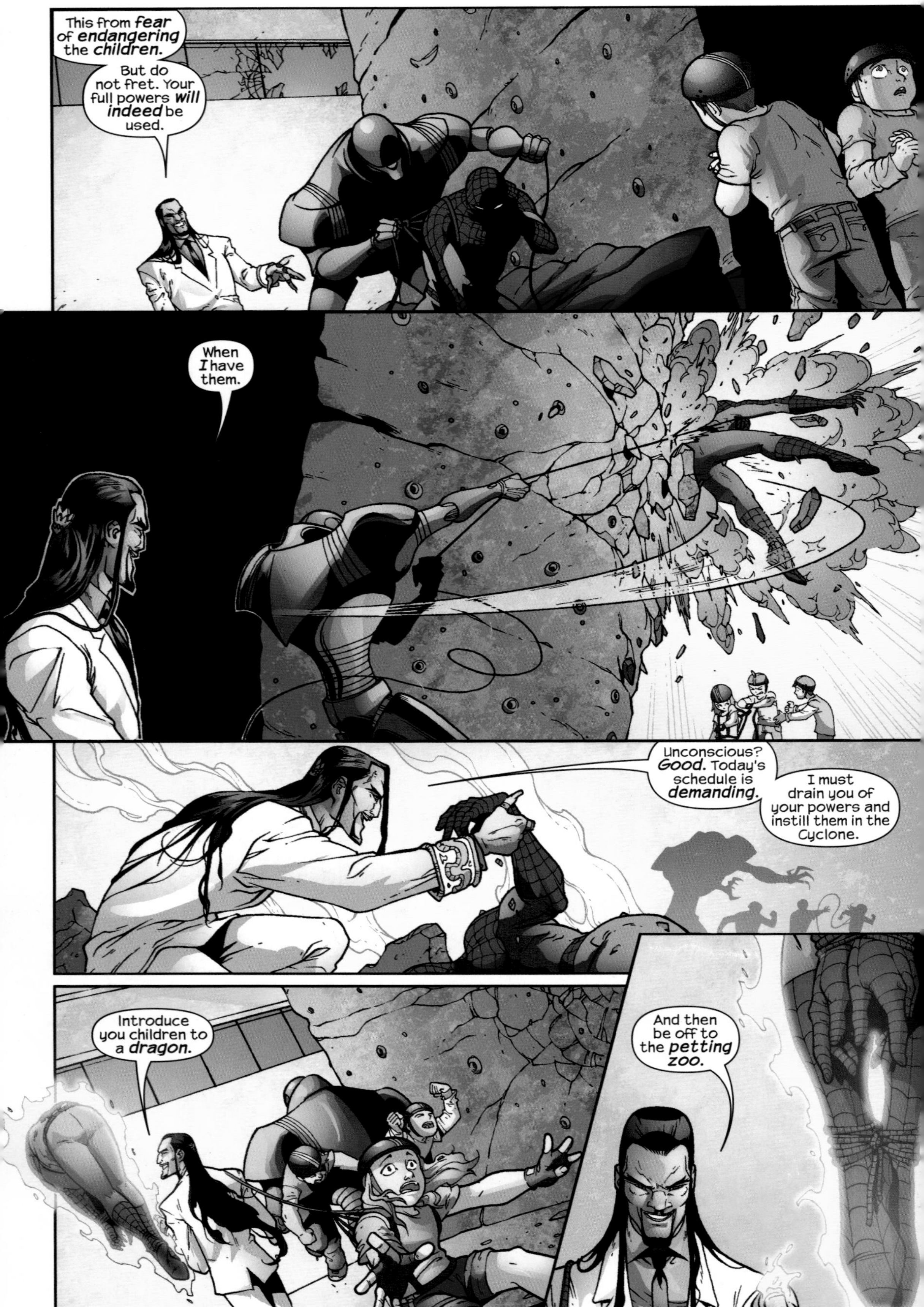
This from *fear* of *endangering* the *children.*
But do not fret. Your full powers ***will indeed*** be used.
When *I* have them.
Unconscious? ***Good.*** Today's schedule is ***demanding.***
I must drain you of your powers and instill them in the Cyclone.
Introduce you children to a ***dragon.***
And then be off to the ***petting zoo.***

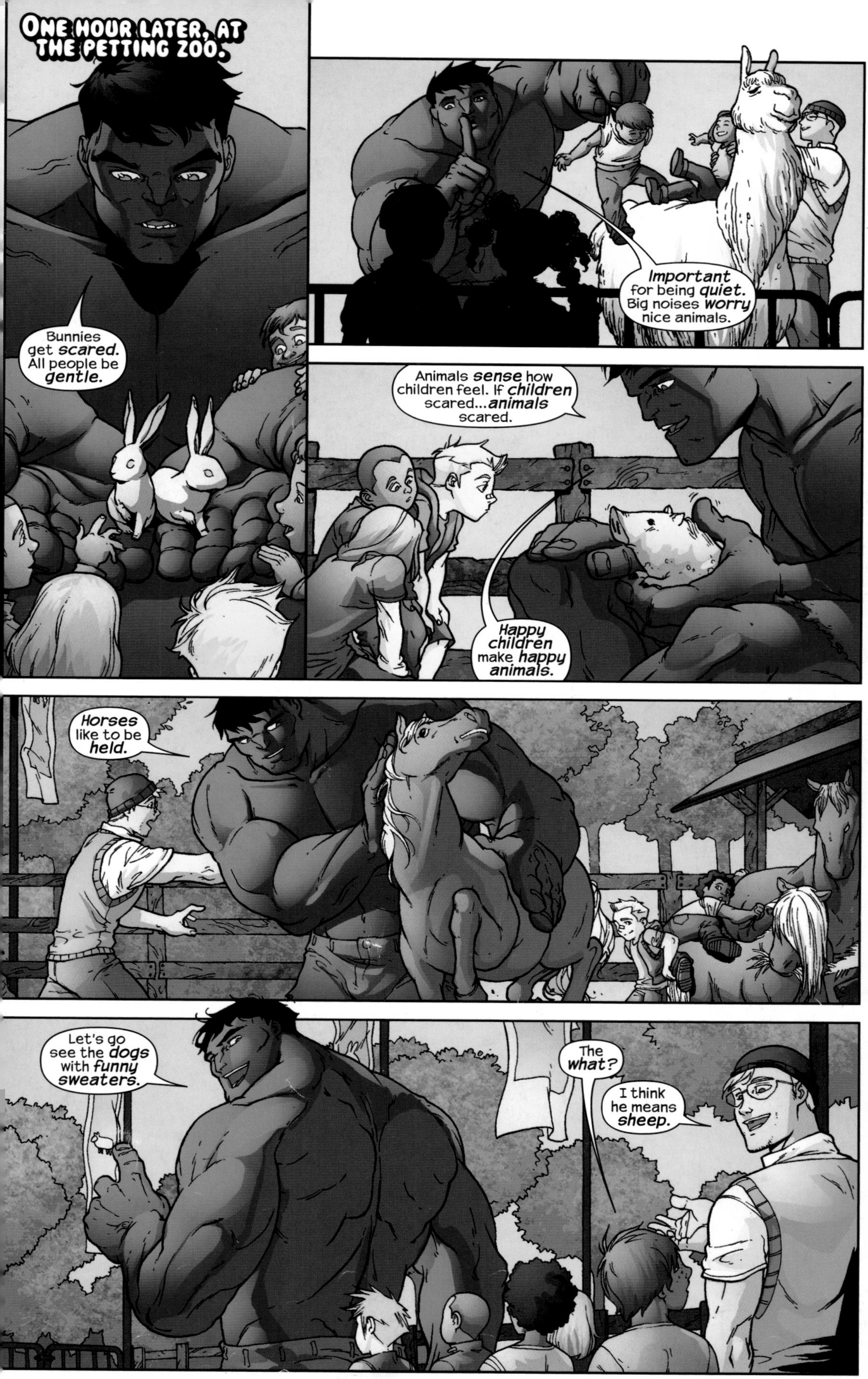
One hour later, at the petting zoo.
Bunnies get scared. All people be gentle.
Important for being quiet. Big noises worry nice animals.
Animals sense how children feel. If children scared...animals scared.
Happy children make happy animals.
Horses like to be held.
Let's go see the dogs with funny sweaters.
The what?
I think he means sheep.

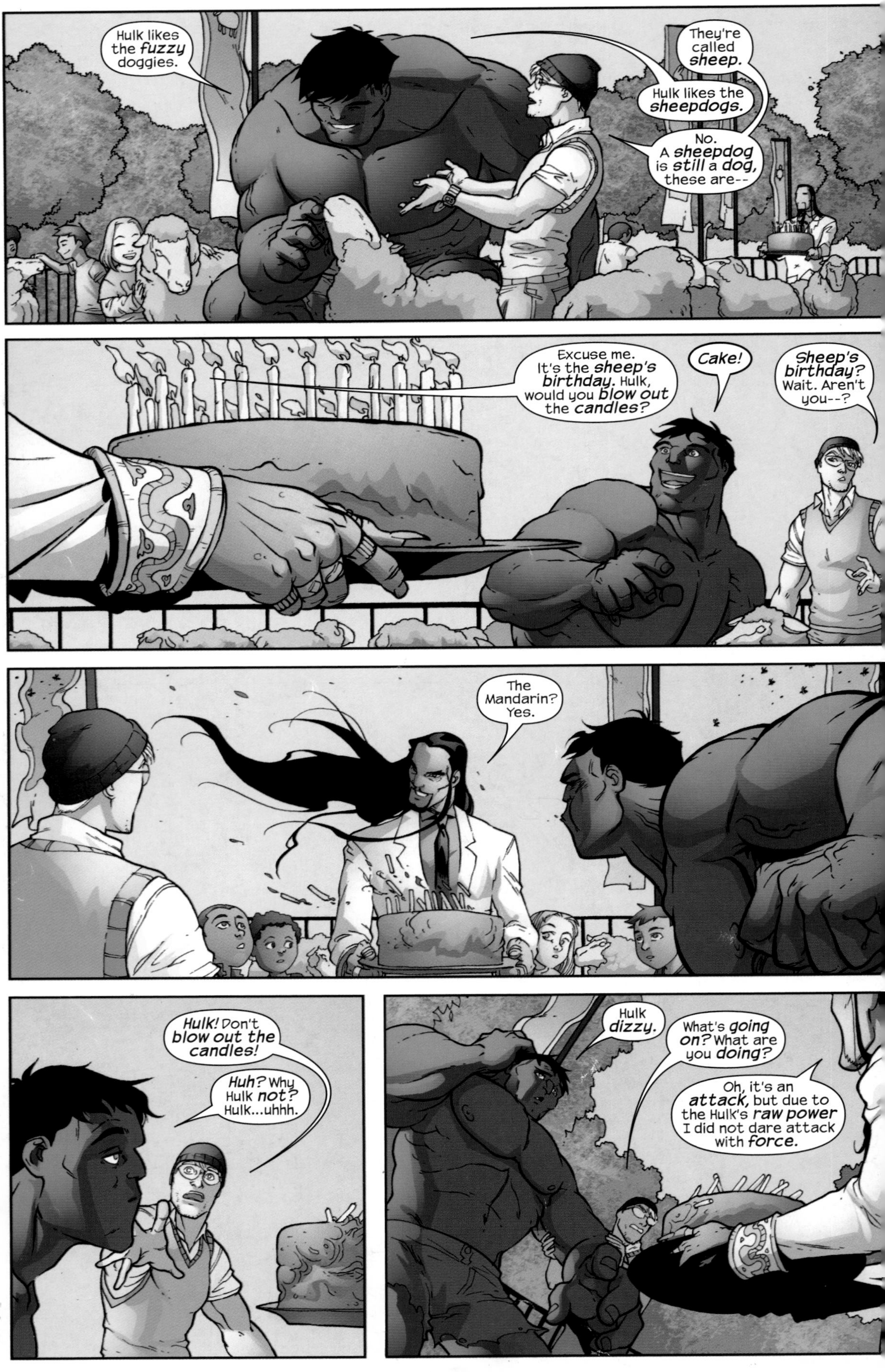
Hulk likes the fuzzy doggies.
They're called sheep.
Hulk likes the sheepdogs.
No. A sheepdog is still a dog, these are--
Excuse me. It's the sheep's birthday. Hulk, would you blow out the candles?
Cake!
Sheep's birthday? Wait. Aren't you--?
The Mandarin? Yes.
Hulk! Don't blow out the candles!
Huh? Why Hulk not? Hulk...uhhh.
Hulk dizzy.
What's going on? What are you doing?
Oh, it's an attack, but due to the Hulk's raw power I did not dare attack with force.

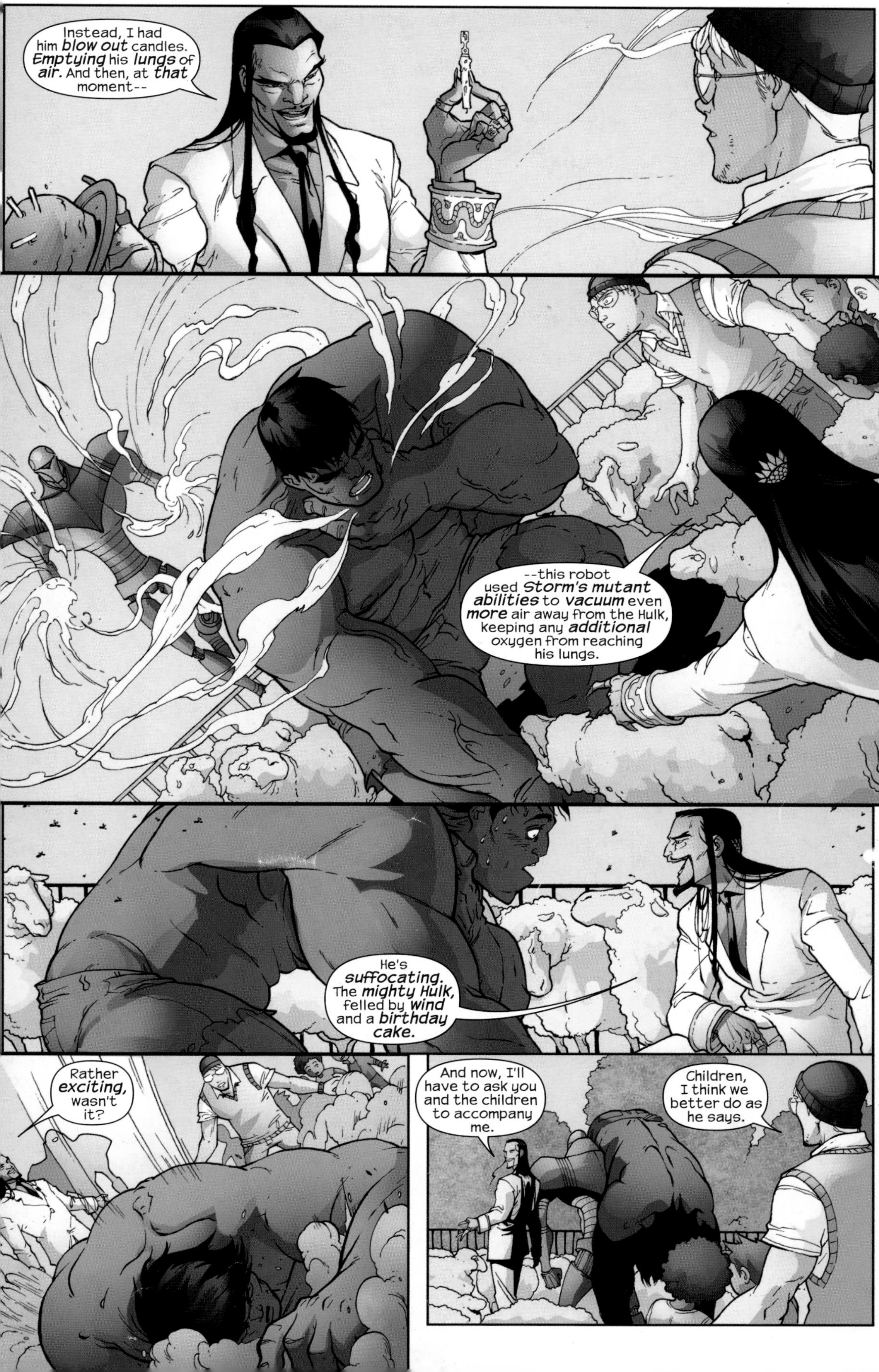
Instead, I had him blow out candles. Emptying his lungs of air. And then, at that moment--
--this robot used Storm's mutant abilities to vacuum even more air away from the Hulk, keeping any additional oxygen from reaching his lungs.
He's suffocating. The mighty Hulk, felled by wind and a birthday cake.
Rather exciting, wasn't it?
And now, I'll have to ask you and the children to accompany me.
Children, I think we better do as he says.

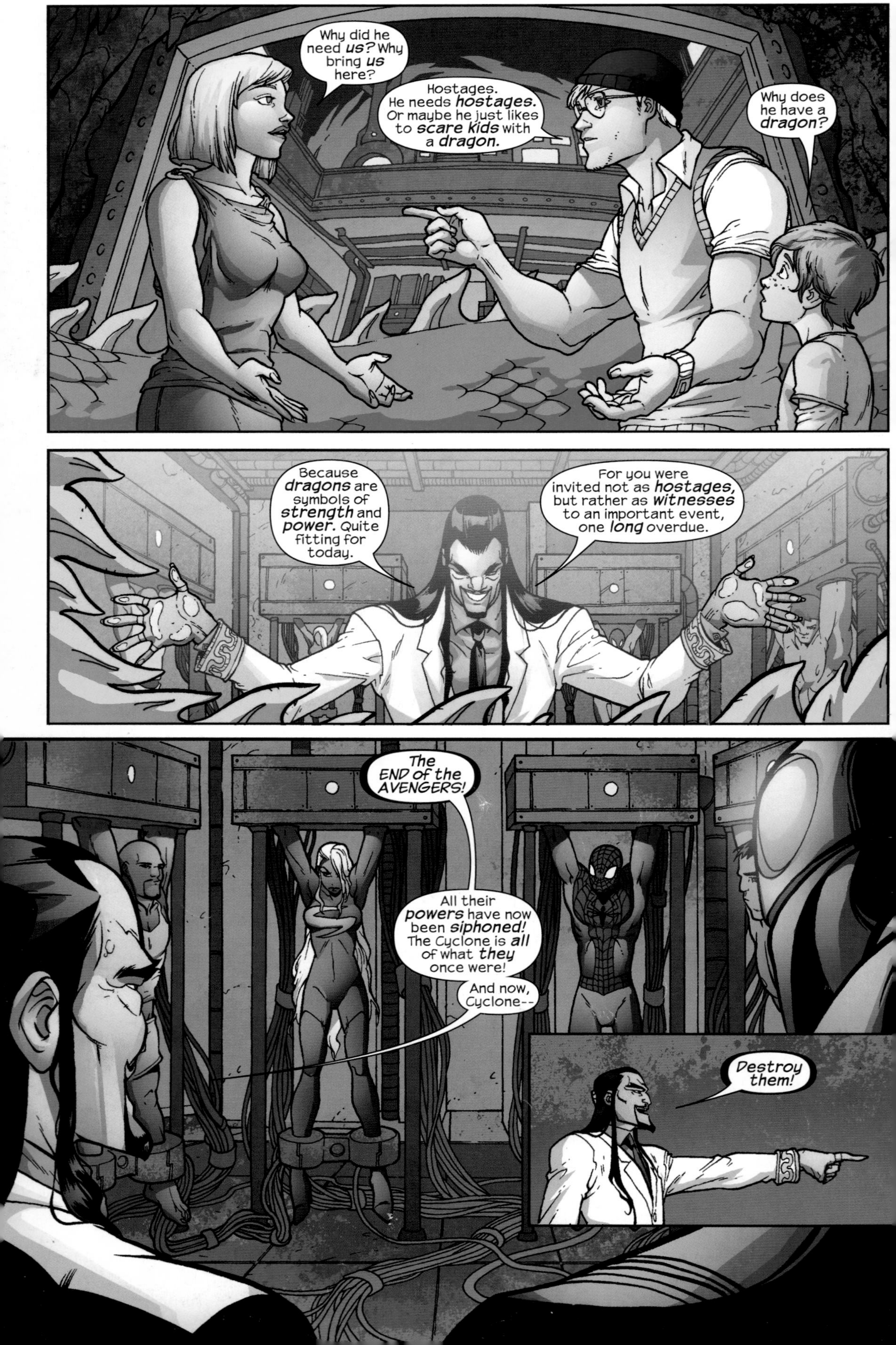

Why did he need us? Why bring us here?
Hostages. He needs hostages. Or maybe he just likes to scare kids with a dragon.
Why does he have a dragon?
Because dragons are symbols of strength and power. Quite fitting for today.
For you were invited not as hostages, but rather as witnesses to an important event, one long overdue.
The END of the AVENGERS!
All their powers have now been siphoned! The Cyclone is all of what they once were!
And now, Cyclone--
Destroy them!

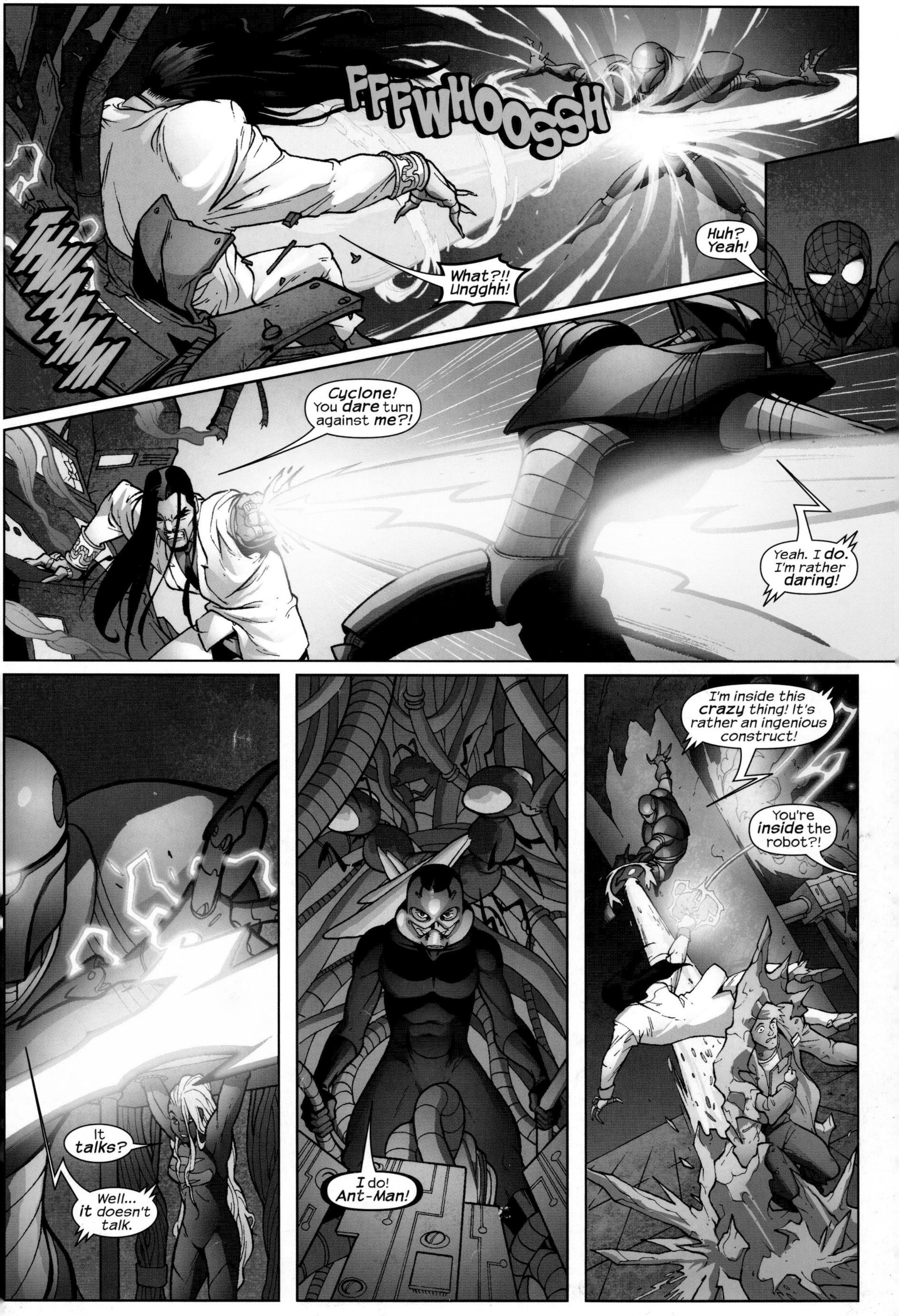
FFFWHOOSSH
THWAAMM
What?!! Ungghh!
Huh? Yeah!
Cyclone! You dare turn against me?!
Yeah. I do. I'm rather daring!
It talks?
Well... it doesn't talk.
I do! Ant-Man!
I'm inside this crazy thing! It's rather an ingenious construct!
You're inside the robot?!

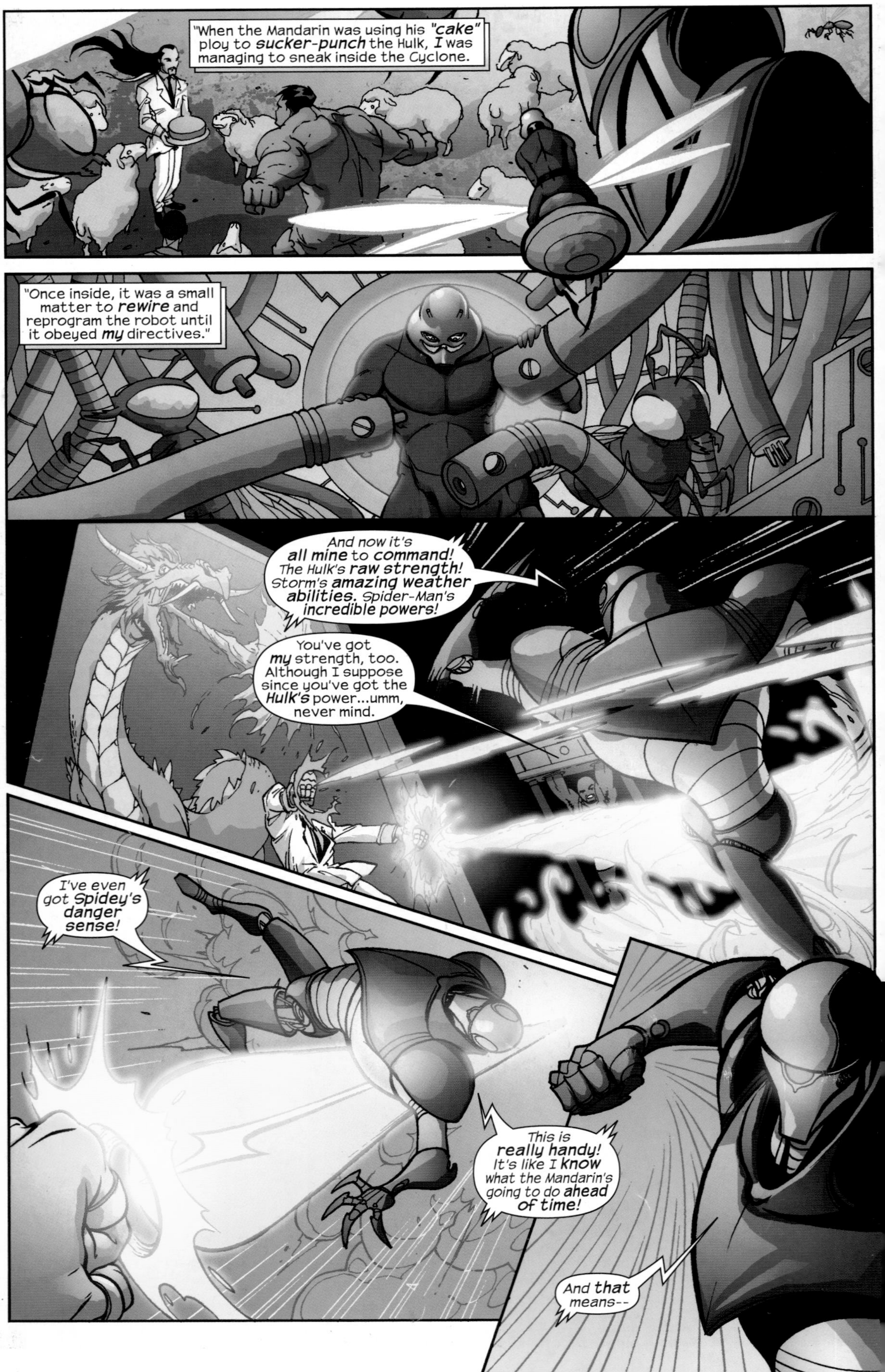
"When the Mandarin was using his "cake" ploy to sucker-punch the Hulk, I was managing to sneak inside the Cyclone.
"Once inside, it was a small matter to rewire and reprogram the robot until it obeyed my directives."
And now it's all mine to command! The Hulk's raw strength! Storm's amazing weather abilities. Spider-Man's incredible powers!
You've got my strength, too. Although I suppose since you've got the Hulk's power...umm, never mind.
I've even got Spidey's danger sense!
This is really handy! It's like I know what the Mandarin's going to do ahead of time!
And that means--

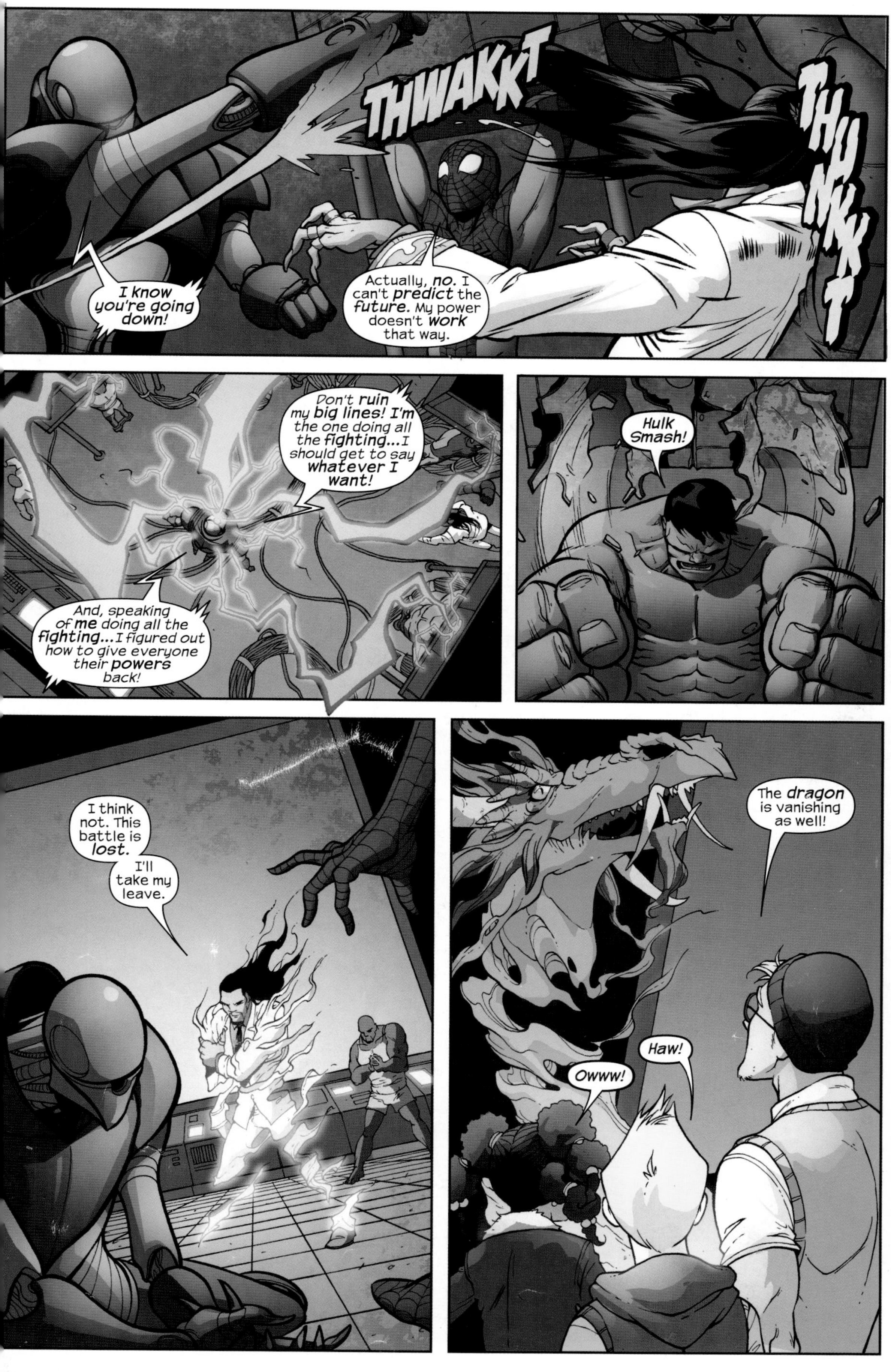
THWAKKT
THUNKKT
I know you're going down!
Actually, no. I can't predict the future. My power doesn't work that way.
Don't ruin my big lines! I'm the one doing all the fighting... I should get to say whatever I want!
And, speaking of me doing all the fighting... I figured out how to give everyone their powers back!
Hulk Smash!
I think not. This battle is lost.
I'll take my leave.
The dragon is vanishing as well!
Haw!
Owww!

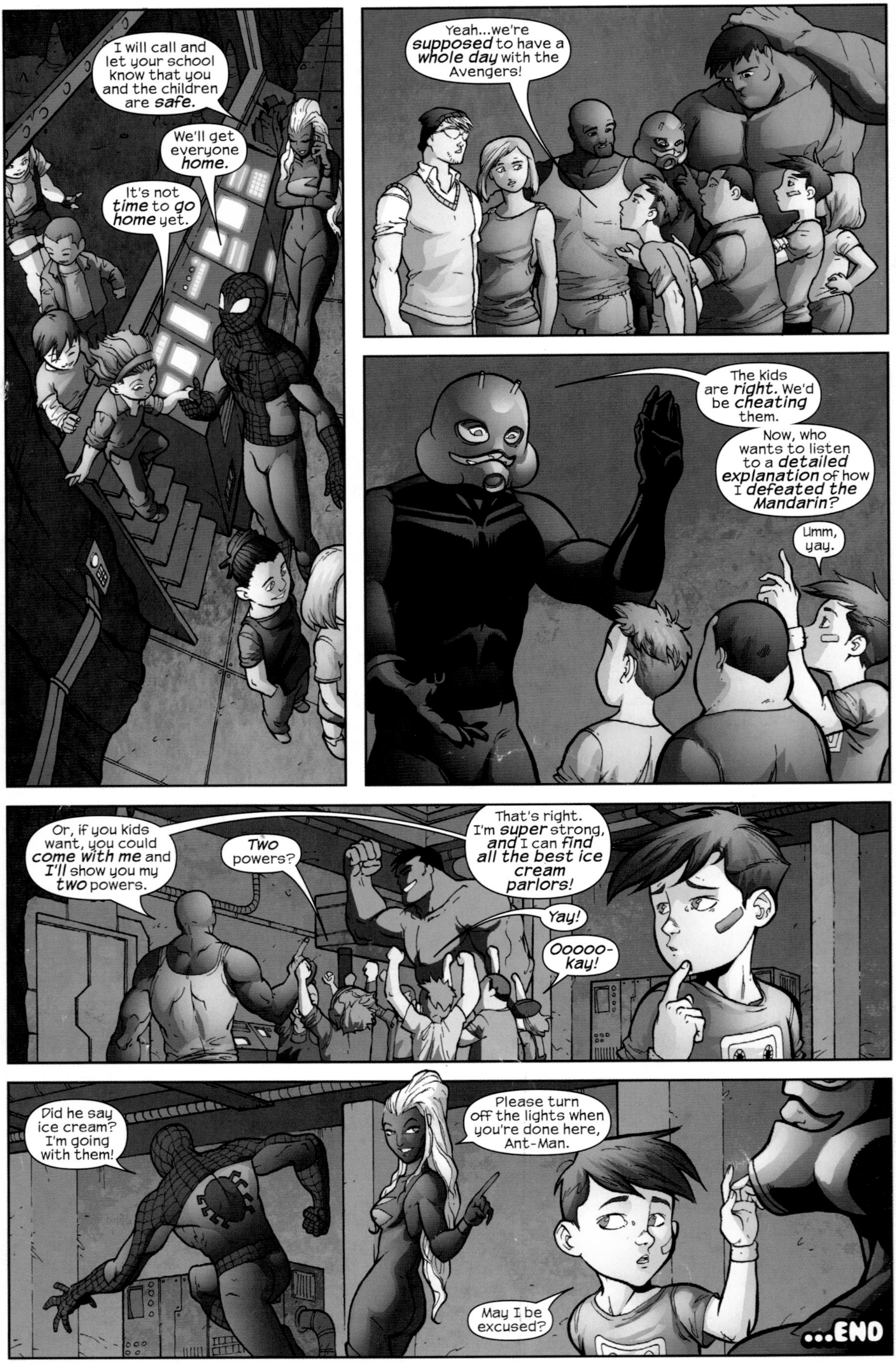
I will call and let your school know that you and the children are *safe.*
We'll get everyone *home.*
It's not *time* to *go home* yet.
Yeah...we're *supposed* to have a *whole day* with the Avengers!
The kids are *right.* We'd be *cheating* them.
Now, who wants to listen to a *detailed explanation* of how I *defeated the Mandarin?*
Umm, yay.
Or, if you kids want, you could *come with me* and *I'll* show you my *two* powers.
Two powers?
That's right. I'm *super* strong, *and* I can *find all the best ice cream parlors!*
Yay!
Ooooo-kay!
Did he say ice cream? I'm going with them!
Please turn off the lights when you're done here, Ant-Man.
May I be excused?
...END